CRASH!

Elizabeth sat down on a big branch and looked around. From up in the tree, she could see the roof of Amy's house. A breeze was blowing. "It's nice up here," she said.

Suddenly, there was a loud cracking sound. Elizabeth looked at the branch she was sitting on. It was starting to break.

"Elizabeth, move!" Amy yelled.

"Give me your hand," Jessica told her sister.

Elizabeth started to inch toward Jessica. But it was too late. With another loud CRACK, the branch broke. Elizabeth slipped, crashed through the lower branches, and fell all the way to the ground.

Bantam Skylark Books in the SWEET VALLEY KIDS series

SWEET VALLEY KIDS

ELIZABETH'S BROKEN ARM

Written by
Molly Mia Stewart

Created by
FRANCINE PASCAL

Illustrated by
Ying-Hwa Hu

A BANTAM SKYLARK BOOK®
NEW YORK • TORONTO • LONDON • SYDNEY • AUCKLAND

RL 2, 005–008

ELIZABETH'S BROKEN ARM
A Bantam Skylark Book / January 1993

Sweet Valley High® and Sweet Valley Kids are trademarks of
Francine Pascal

Conceived by Francine Pascal

Produced by Daniel Weiss Associates, Inc.
33 West 17th Street
New York, NY 10011

Cover art by Susan Tang

Skylark Books is a registered trademark of Bantam Books, a division
of Bantam Doubleday Dell Publishing Group, Inc. Registered in U.S.
Patent and Trademark Office and elsewhere.

ISBN 0-553-48009-X

Published simultaneously in the United States and Canada

Bantam Books are published by Bantam Books, a division of Bantam
Doubleday Dell Publishing Group, Inc. Its trademark, consisting of the
words "Bantam Books" and the portrayal of a rooster, is Registered in
U.S. Patent and Trademark Office and in other countries. Marca Regis-
trada. Bantam Books, 666 Fifth Avenue, New York, New York 10103.

PRINTED IN THE UNITED STATES OF AMERICA

CWO   0 9 8 7 6 5 4 3 2 1

To Melodie Joy Kauff

CHAPTER 1

A Big Announcement

"What kinds of animals is she going to bring?" Jessica Wakefield asked her teacher, Mrs. Otis, on Monday morning.

Mrs. Otis had just told her second-grade class that a zookeeper from the Sweet Valley Zoo was going to visit them the following Monday. Everyone was excited.

"The zookeeper, Alice Costello, is going to bring three animals," the teacher said, looking down at a letter from the zoo. "There'll be a snake called a boa constrictor, a tarantula spider, and a baby leopard."

"Wow!" said Jessica's twin sister, Elizabeth. "All the animals are so different."

"Will we be able to pet them?" Winston Egbert asked. Winston was the skinniest boy in the class, and his ears stuck out.

"Yes," Mrs. Otis replied.

"Even the snake?" Eva Simpson asked.

"Even the snake," Mrs. Otis told her.

Jessica had seen a boa constrictor at the zoo, but she didn't know what a tarantula spider looked like. She wasn't sure she wanted to, either. There were lots of spiders in her yard at home, and she didn't like them at all. She definitely was looking forward to seeing the leopard, though. She'd never seen one up close.

"The zookeeper will need a special helper while she's here," Mrs. Otis went on. "She asked me to pick one person to be her assistant."

Jessica's hand shot up. "Please, Mrs. Otis. I'll do a good job."

2

"So will I," Caroline Pearce called out. "Pick me!"

"No, *me*," Kisho Murasaki yelled.

"I want to help," Lila Fowler shouted.

Mrs. Otis laughed. Every student in the class had raised his or her hand. "It's too hard for me to choose one person all by myself," she said. "We'll have to have a contest."

Jessica smiled. She loved contests, especially when she won.

Mrs. Otis turned around and picked up a piece of chalk. Then she began to list the names of everyone in the class on the front blackboard.

Jessica and Elizabeth leaned close to each other. "This is great," they whispered at exactly the same time. Then they both giggled. Jessica and Elizabeth often said things at exactly the same time. That's because they were identical twins.

Jessica and Elizabeth looked exactly alike.

They both had blue-green eyes and long, blond hair with bangs. In school they sat next to each other, and they shared a bedroom at home. When they wore matching outfits, even their closest friends had trouble telling them apart without looking at the name bracelets the twins always wore.

But even though they looked the same on the outside, Jessica and Elizabeth were very different on the inside. Elizabeth was a high scorer for her team in the Sweet Valley Soccer League, while Jessica didn't even like playing soccer. Elizabeth loved school and always did her homework right away, while Jessica groaned and complained when she had to open her schoolbooks.

But Jessica and Elizabeth didn't let their differences stop them from being best friends. They knew they would be best friends forever.

Mrs. Otis finished writing the list of names.

She turned to face the class. "Did I forget anyone?"

"No," several kids yelled.

"Good," Mrs. Otis said. She turned back to the board, put down the white chalk, and picked up some blue chalk. Then she began to draw ten stars next to each name. Jessica felt impatient. She wondered when Mrs. Otis was going to tell them about the contest.

Finally, Mrs. Otis finished drawing the stars. She turned to face the class. "This is how the contest will work. Everyone has ten stars. You'll lose one star if you are absent or late, one star if you don't have your homework, and one star if I hear you talking or whispering when you ought to be working. The person who has the most stars on Friday wins."

"What if two people have the same number of stars left?" Amy Sutton asked. Amy was Elizabeth's best friend after Jessica.

6

"If two or more people have the same number of stars when the final bell rings on Friday, I'll ask them a question about zoos," Mrs. Otis said. "Whoever gives the correct or best answer wins." The teacher paused. "Any other questions?"

Nobody raised a hand.

"OK," Mrs. Otis said. "The contest starts now."

Jessica and Elizabeth looked at each other and smiled. Jessica wanted to tell Elizabeth that she thought the contest was going to be fun, but she didn't. She knew that if she whispered, she would lose a star. It was going to be hard to be good until Friday.

CHAPTER 2

The Elephant Tree

"Six more days until the zookeeper comes," Elizabeth said.

It was after school the next day. Elizabeth and Jessica were going to Amy's house to play.

"I wish I could be the assistant zookeeper," Amy said with a frown.

Elizabeth and Jessica knew why Amy was sad. She had been late to school and had forgotten to bring in her homework. Mrs. Otis had erased two of her stars. Amy only had eight left.

"You still might win," Jessica told her.

"Maybe," Amy said, but she didn't sound very hopeful.

Jessica grinned. "At least you're not in last place."

Amy, Jessica, and Elizabeth laughed. Jessica *was* in last place. She was tied with Ellen Riteman. Jessica and Ellen had gotten caught whispering four times since yesterday. They each had only six stars left.

"Lila might win," Elizabeth pointed out. Lila was Jessica's best friend after Elizabeth, and she was in second place. She had been whispering with Jessica and Ellen all four times, but Mrs. Otis had only caught her once. Lila still had nine stars.

"Andy has a good chance of winning," Jessica added. "So does Caroline. They never whisper or do anything to get in trouble."

Caroline Pearce and Andy Franklin each had nine stars, just like Lila.

9

"I think you'll beat them, Elizabeth," Amy said.

"I hope so," Elizabeth said with a smile. She was in first place because she still had all ten of her stars.

"I'll race you," Jessica called out. "Last one to Amy's front door is a rotten egg!" Amy, Jessica, and Elizabeth started to run toward Amy's house.

Jessica and Elizabeth ran as fast as they could, but Amy got to her front door first. "I win," she yelled.

Amy's father opened the door just after Amy tagged it. He was a photographer and had come back that morning from an out-of-town assignment for a magazine.

"What's the hurry?" Mr. Sutton asked with a smile. "Do you have ants in your pants?"

"No," Amy answered, giggling. "We're starving!"

"Then I'd better make you a snack right

away," Mr. Sutton said. He led the way to the kitchen.

Amy, Jessica, and Elizabeth each drank a glass of milk and ate a piece of carrot cake. Then Amy jumped to her feet. "Come on," she said. "Let's climb my new favorite tree."

Amy led the twins out to her backyard and ran to a tall tree with dark purple leaves. The bark on the tree's trunk was gray and wrinkled.

"I call this the elephant tree," Amy told Jessica and Elizabeth. "Can you guess why?"

"I know," Jessica said. "It's because the trunk looks like an elephant's leg."

Amy nodded. "Right." She walked under the tree, and Jessica and Elizabeth followed her. "The branches grow close together," Amy added. "So it's easy to climb. I'll show you."

Amy put a foot on one of the low branches and started climbing up. Soon she was above

11

the twins' heads. "It's really easy," she called down. "Come on up."

Elizabeth and Jessica looked at each other. They both liked to climb trees too. In fact, they had climbed so many of them, they were experts.

"Let's go," Elizabeth said. She scooted up the tree like a monkey. Jessica was close behind. Soon the twins were as high as Amy.

Elizabeth sat down on a big branch and looked around. From up in the tree, she could see the roof of Amy's house. A breeze was blowing. "It's nice up here," she said.

Suddenly, there was a loud cracking sound. Elizabeth looked at the branch she was sitting on. It was starting to break.

"Elizabeth, move!" Amy yelled.

Elizabeth's eyes widened. "I can't."

"Give me your hand," Jessica told her sister.

Elizabeth started to inch toward Jessica. But it was too late. With another loud CRACK, the branch broke. Elizabeth slipped, crashed through the lower branches, and fell all the way to the ground.

CHAPTER 3

Emergency!

Jessica's heart pounded. "Liz, are you OK?" she shouted as she scrambled down the tree. Amy climbed down right behind her.

When they got to the ground, Amy and Jessica found Elizabeth sitting under the tree. She was holding her left arm with her right one and crying hard.

"Are you OK, Liz?" Jessica asked again, sitting down next to her sister on the ground. Elizabeth was crying too hard to talk. She just shook her head.

"You'd better go get help," Jessica told Amy.

Amy nodded and ran toward the house.

Jessica patted Elizabeth on the back. "Don't worry, Liz. I'm here. You'll be OK."

Elizabeth kept crying. But she nodded.

A few seconds later, Amy came running back out with her father.

Mr. Sutton knelt down next to Elizabeth. "Tell me what hurts."

"My arm," Elizabeth sobbed. "It hurts a lot."

"Can you move it?" Mr. Sutton asked.

"No," Elizabeth said, tears streaming down her cheeks.

Mr. Sutton looked worried. "Elizabeth, it looks as though your arm is starting to swell. Don't be afraid. We're going to take you to the hospital so that a doctor can look at it. We'll go as soon as I call your mother. OK?"

Elizabeth nodded.

"Good," Mr. Sutton said. "Stay right here."

A few minutes later, Mr. Sutton helped Elizabeth into the backseat of the Suttons' car.

Jessica climbed in after her. Amy got into the front seat.

Jessica held Elizabeth's unhurt hand. She felt awful that her sister was in pain and there was nothing she could do to make her feel better.

"Are we almost at the hospital?" Jessica asked. She wanted Mr. Sutton to go faster.

Mr. Sutton looked at Jessica and Elizabeth in the rearview mirror. "Another turn and we'll be there," he said. He turned onto a street and then into a driveway, where a big sign said EMERGENCY ROOM.

Mrs. Wakefield was waiting for them inside. She was talking to a nurse and writing something on a piece of paper.

"Mom!" Jessica called. "Over here."

Mrs. Wakefield rushed over to the twins and took Elizabeth's good hand. "It's all right, honey. Everything will be fine."

"I feel terrible about what happened," Mr. Sutton spoke up.

Mrs. Wakefield gave him a worried smile. "These things happen. No one is to blame." She looked down at Elizabeth. "We can go see the doctor now. He'll make you all better." She turned to Jessica. "Stay here with Mr. Sutton, Jessica. Elizabeth and I will be back out soon."

Jessica watched as the nurse led Mrs. Wakefield and Elizabeth through a swinging door. Soon she couldn't see them anymore.

"What do we do now?" Jessica asked, looking up at Mr. Sutton.

"We have to wait," Mr. Sutton answered.

The hospital had a special waiting area. It was filled with magazines, books, and toys. It even had a slide in one corner made out of bright red, blue, and yellow plastic.

"Want to play on the slide?" Amy asked Jessica.

Jessica shook her head. "I don't feel like it. I'm too worried."

"Hospitals aren't much fun," Mr. Sutton said. "For the patient or for visitors."

"You're right," Jessica agreed. "Elizabeth and I got our tonsils taken out here. We stayed in the hospital for a few days."

"I remember," Amy said. "Some boys snuck in their pet turtles, right?"

Jessica smiled a little bit. "That's right." She looked at the clock on the wall. "I hate waiting," she said.

Finally Elizabeth appeared through the swinging door. Jessica ran over and gave her a big hug.

Elizabeth hugged her back. She was smiling. Mrs. Wakefield was smiling too. Jessica looked at Elizabeth's arm.

"You got a cast," Jessica said. "That's so cool!"

"Excellent," Amy agreed. "Does that mean your arm is broken?"

"Yes," Elizabeth said. She showed Jessica, Amy, and Mr. Sutton an X-ray the doctor had taken of her arm. They could see her bone, and the place where it was broken.

Elizabeth also showed Jessica and Amy a special pen the nurse had given her. "You can change the tip so that the pen writes in different colors," Elizabeth explained. "It's made just for writing on casts."

"I want to sign your cast," Amy said.

"Me too," Jessica said.

"OK." Elizabeth smiled. "You can go first, Jessica."

Jessica chose a red tip and wrote, "Get well soon, from your very best friend." She drew a big red heart around it.

When Elizabeth read that, she smiled again.

Next, Amy wrote something.

21

"I can't read it," Elizabeth told Amy. "It's upside down."

"It says, 'I'm sorry about the tree,'" Amy said quietly.

"Don't feel bad," Elizabeth told her. "You didn't know the branch was going to break. Besides, I like my cast."

Jessica did too. She almost wished *she* had been the one to fall out of the tree—but not quite.

CHAPTER 4

Elizabeth's Boring Day

"Please?" Elizabeth said. "I want to go."
It was Wednesday morning at breakfast. Mrs. Wakefield had just announced that Elizabeth had to stay home from school.

Steven, the twins' older brother, was eating his second bowl of cereal. "How about if *I* stay home? I don't mind."

Jessica pretended not to hear Steven. "Elizabeth feels much better. Please let her come to school."

"Sorry, girls," Mrs. Wakefield said. "Doctor's orders. Elizabeth's arm has a lot of healing to do." Mrs. Wakefield put a hand on Elizabeth's head. "Your arm needs rest, honey."

"But, Mom," Elizabeth said. "My arm doesn't hurt today. And if I'm absent, I'll lose a star."

Jessica nodded. "That means Elizabeth might lose her chance to help the zookeeper."

"I'm sorry. I know how important that is to you, Elizabeth," Mrs. Wakefield said. "But it's more important for you to get well. Now, no more arguing. Jessica, run upstairs and get ready. The bus will be here soon."

Jessica and Elizabeth walked up to their room. Elizabeth sat on her bed while Jessica pulled a pink shirt out of their closet.

"School won't be any fun without you," Jessica said as she got dressed.

"Staying home won't be any fun without you," Elizabeth said.

Soon Jessica and Steven left for school. After they had gone, Elizabeth lay down on her bed and read a library book called *Animals in the Zoo.*

When Elizabeth finished the book, she carried it downstairs and looked at the clock in the kitchen. The big hand was between the eight and the nine. The little hand was on the eight.

Elizabeth couldn't believe it. It was only twenty minutes before nine.

Elizabeth read *Animals in the Zoo* again. When she finished, the clock said five minutes before nine.

Elizabeth listened to the clock go *tick, tock, tick, tock.*

Six more hours until Jessica comes home, Elizabeth told herself.

Tick, tock, said the clock. *Tick, tock. Tick, tock.*

"Staying home from school is boring," Elizabeth said out loud. She imagined Jessica at school, laughing with their friends and having fun on the playground. Then Elizabeth imagined Mrs. Otis announcing that Lila would be the assistant zookeeper.

Elizabeth felt grumpy. "Breaking my arm is the dumbest thing I've ever done," she muttered. She got up and went looking for her mother. Mrs. Wakefield was taking a load of clothes out of the dryer.

"Mom," Elizabeth whined. "My arm hurts."

"Poor dear," Mrs. Wakefield said, brushing Elizabeth's hair out of her eyes. "Would you like to go upstairs and take a nap?"

Just then the doorbell rang. Elizabeth ran to get it. Mrs. Wakefield followed her. Elizabeth threw open the door.

A man was standing on the porch. He was holding a big bunch of red, blue, green, and orange balloons.

"Is Miss Elizabeth Wakefield at home?" the man asked.

"I'm Elizabeth Wakefield," Elizabeth said.

"Then these are for you," the man said, handing Elizabeth the balloons. "But be careful. I wouldn't want you to float away."

"Don't worry," Elizabeth said, giggling. "I have my cast to hold me down." She held up her arm so the man could see.

Mrs. Wakefield thanked the delivery man. Then she helped Elizabeth squeeze the balloons through the door.

"Who are they from?" Elizabeth asked.

"Let me look," Mrs. Wakefield said. She found a card taped to one of the yellow balloons and handed it to Elizabeth.

"Get well soon," Elizabeth read. "With love from the Suttons."

"How thoughtful," Mrs. Wakefield said. "I know Amy and her parents feel awful about what happened."

Elizabeth smiled as she lifted her right hand up so the balloons almost reached the ceiling. "I bet this was Amy's idea. The balloons are great. Don't you think so, Mom?"

"Absolutely," Mrs. Wakefield said with a smile. "So, how about that nap?"

Elizabeth wrinkled her nose. "I don't think I need a nap. My arm feels much better now."

Mrs. Wakefield laughed. "Then how about helping me make some cookies?"

"Yummy," Elizabeth said. "I'll put the balloons in my room, and then I'll be right down. Can we make chocolate-chip-peanut-butter cookies?"

"Anything you want," Mrs. Wakefield said.

When Elizabeth got back downstairs, her mother had already taken the flour, baking soda, sugar, peanut butter, and chocolate chips out of a cupboard.

Elizabeth took the eggs and butter out of the refrigerator. "I'm glad I stayed home. Otherwise, I wouldn't have been here to get my balloons."

"And I wouldn't have someone to bake—" Mrs. Wakefield began.

But she didn't get a chance to finish her sentence because the doorbell rang again.

"Should I get it?" Elizabeth asked. She saw that her mother's hands were covered with flour.

"You might as well." Mrs. Wakefield smiled at Elizabeth. "I have a feeling it's for you."

CHAPTER 5

Jessica's Horrible Day

While Elizabeth was having fun making cookies at home, Jessica was having a miserable time at school. Mrs. Otis had just asked everyone to pick a partner for a special art project.

Jessica looked at Elizabeth's empty desk and frowned. She and Elizabeth almost always worked together on projects.

Who am I going to work with now? Jessica wondered. She looked over at Lila, but Ellen was already moving her chair toward Lila's desk. She glanced around the room. Eva was sitting next to Amy. Julie Porter was sitting with Caroline Pearce. Suzie Nichols was sitting with Sandy Ferris. All of Jessica's friends had someone to work with.

"Do you have a partner, Jessica?" Mrs. Otis asked.

Jessica's face turned red. She shook her head.

"Who else doesn't have a partner yet?" Mrs. Otis called out.

Winston Egbert raised his hand.

"OK, Jessica," Mrs. Otis said. "Team up with Winston. You can move your chair over to his desk."

Jessica felt embarrassed. Not having a partner was terrible. But being partners with a boy—especially Winston—was worse. Winston liked to goof off and play jokes on people.

"But, Mrs. Otis . . ." Jessica complained.

"Go on," Mrs. Otis told her. "Winston won't bite you."

"That's what you think," Todd Wilkins called out. Everyone laughed, including Winston.

Jessica didn't laugh, though. She slowly got up and dragged her chair toward Winston's desk. But she didn't get too close. Winston's desk was messy. He had drawn airplanes all over it with his pencil.

"Howdy, partner," Winston said, looking up at Jessica as she sat down. He had flipped his eyelids up so that the red underside showed.

Jessica jumped back in surprise. "Gross! Mrs. Otis, Winston is disgusting. Make him stop!"

"Winston," Mrs. Otis said. "Partners aren't for teasing. Please work with Jessica nicely."

Winston stuck out his tongue at Jessica. "Tattletale," he whispered.

Jessica pretended not to see or hear him.

But Winston wouldn't leave Jessica alone.

He teased her all morning while the class made Get Well cards for Elizabeth.

Jessica was happy when the lunch bell rang. She was starving. But when she looked for her lunch bag, she couldn't find it.

"Hurry up, Jessica," Lila said from the doorway. "Or someone else will get our favorite table."

"Yeah, come on," Ellen said. "What are you doing?"

"Looking for my lunch," Jessica answered. "I think I forgot it." Elizabeth always reminded Jessica to grab her lunch from the counter before they left together for school. So Jessica felt a little bit angry with Elizabeth, even though she wasn't really to blame.

"It's all right, Jessica," Mrs. Otis said from her desk. She took her wallet out of her purse and handed Jessica enough money to buy a hot lunch. "Here you go."

Jessica thanked Mrs. Otis and hurried to

the cafeteria with her friends. She loved to eat and gossip. But when Jessica got in line for food, she felt like crying.

The cafeteria was serving meat loaf and creamed corn—two of Jessica's least favorite foods. Lunchtime was going to be just as bad as the morning.

Things didn't get any better after lunch, either. Jessica didn't smile until the final bell rang. Then she skipped all the way to the bus, climbed aboard, and sat down in the seat she and Elizabeth always shared. The worst day in the history of the world was almost over, she thought.

But that's when Charlie Cashman sat down next to Jessica. Charlie's friend Jerry McAllister sat in front of Charlie. Jerry and Charlie were the biggest bullies in Mrs. Otis's class.

"You can't sit here," Jessica said.

"Why not?" Charlie asked. "It's empty."

Jessica frowned. "Because that's Elizabeth's seat."

"So what?" Charlie said, leaning back and putting his hands behind his head. "Elizabeth is absent today."

Jessica looked around the bus for another seat she could move to. Someone was sitting next to her brother, and there weren't any empty seats next to girls. Jessica sighed. She was stuck. *Why did Elizabeth have to break her arm?* she thought grumpily. *It's all her fault I'm having such a bad day.*

"Eww," Charlie said. "Jessica, you're sititng on a huge piece of gooey gum."

Jessica jumped up. "Did I get it on me?" She looked down at the seat and saw that there wasn't any gum there at all.

Charlie and Jerry burst into laughter.

Jessica fell back into her seat. She looked out the window and pretended Charlie and Jerry were invisible.

When the bus got to Jessica's stop, Charlie wouldn't move so she could get by. Jessica had to climb over him. And then Jerry pulled her hair as she walked past.

Jessica stomped down the aisle, jumped off the bus, and started to run home.

"Hey, what's the big rush?" Steven yelled after her.

Jessica didn't answer. She couldn't wait to tell Elizabeth about her terrible day. Jessica knew Elizabeth would cheer her up.

"Hi, Jessica," Elizabeth said as soon as her sister walked in the door. "Look what I got— candy from Grandma and Grandpa, flowers from Aunt Nancy and Uncle Kirk, and a huge bunch of balloons from Amy's mom and dad!"

Jessica handed Elizabeth a large envelope. "Here are some cards from everyone at school."

"Wow," Elizabeth said with a big smile. "Neat."

Instead of making Jessica feel better, Elizabeth was making her feel worse. Jessica was having the worst day in the history of the world and Elizabeth was getting presents.

"What happened with the contest?" Elizabeth asked as she opened the envelope and started reading the cards.

"Caroline and Amy were talking during math," Jessica told her. "They each lost a star. Andy was late. He's down to seven."

"How about Lila?" Elizabeth wanted to know.

"You two are tied for first place," Jessica said.

Elizabeth frowned. Jessica smiled. She was glad to have bad news for her sister. Elizabeth had already gotten all kinds of great presents, while Jessica had gotten teased all day and had had to eat gross food for lunch. Jessica didn't think her sister deserved any good news right now.

CHAPTER 6

Elizabeth the Hero

"Welcome back, Elizabeth," Amy exclaimed.

"Does your arm hurt?" asked Ellen.

"Can I sign your cast?" said Kisho.

Elizabeth laughed. It was Thursday, her first day back at school. She had just walked into the classroom, and everyone was crowding around to welcome her back. "I want everyone to sign my cast. You can go first, Kisho." She handed him the special cast-signing pen the nurse at the hospital had given her.

Kisho drew a beautiful cat on Elizabeth's cast and signed his name in Japanese under it. Then Todd and Julie signed their names. Next, Lila drew a smiling face and wrote, "Get well soon." Ellen wrote the exact same thing.

"My cast looks great," Elizabeth said. "There's almost no blank space left for people to write."

Amy gave Elizabeth a hug. "Does your arm hurt?"

"A little," Elizabeth admitted.

"Tell us how you fell," Kisho said. "Were you high up in the tree?"

"Yeah," Caroline added. "I want to hear all about it."

Mrs. Otis came up and patted Elizabeth's shoulder. "It's nice to have you back."

Elizabeth grinned. "Thanks."

"Why don't we have a special show-and-tell this morning?" Mrs. Otis suggested. "That way you can tell the whole class what happened. Everyone is very curious."

"OK," Elizabeth agreed.

As soon as Mrs. Otis had taken attendance, Elizabeth walked to the front of the room.

"The day before yesterday," Elizabeth began, "I went to Amy's house to play."

"I was there too," Jessica called out.

"Right," Elizabeth said. "Jessica and I both went to Amy's. After we had a snack, we climbed this big wrinkled tree. I was sitting on a branch way up high, when suddenly I heard a loud CRAACK!"

"It sounded like a baseball bat hitting a ball," Jessica added.

Caroline turned around. "Shh," she said, putting her finger to her lips.

Jessica stuck out her tongue at Caroline.

"The branch was breaking," Elizabeth said. "And—"

"I told Elizabeth to move," Jessica interrupted. "But she was too slow. The branch broke and Elizabeth fell. I was really scared."

"Be quiet," Todd said from his seat behind Jessica. "Elizabeth is telling the story."

"That's right," Amy said. "Elizabeth broke her arm, not you. Let her talk."

"OK, I will," Jessica said huffily. She leaned back in her chair and crossed her arms in front of her chest.

Elizabeth knew Jessica was upset because nobody was listening to her. But she didn't think there was any reason that they should. After all, Jessica wasn't the one who had broken her arm. Elizabeth continued with her story and answered all the questions her classmates asked her. Jessica didn't say another word the whole time. She just sat in her chair, frowning.

Elizabeth smiled at her sister when she got back to her seat, but Jessica looked away. Elizabeth wanted to ask Jessica what was wrong, but she was afraid Mrs. Otis would hear her. Elizabeth and Lila were still tied in the assistant-zookeeper contest, and Elizabeth really wanted to win. Besides, her arm was beginning to hurt and she felt grumpy.

At lunch, Elizabeth waited for Jessica to sit next to her, but Jessica sat between Lila and Ellen at the other end of the table. And at recess, when Jessica saw that Elizabeth was playing marbles with Amy and Eva, she went over and started a game of jump rope with Lila and Ellen at the other end of the playground.

"Is something bugging Jessica?" Amy asked Elizabeth. "She's not talking to you."

Elizabeth shrugged. "I guess she's just mad

44

because I'm the center of attention and she's not."

"Well, she should be extra nice to you now, not extra mean," Eva said.

Elizabeth looked sad as she glanced over at Jessica. "I know."

CHAPTER 7

Lila in the Lead

"Come here, Elizabeth," Amy called from the back of the classroom the next morning. She was feeding the class hamsters, Tinkerbell and Thumbelina, before the first bell rang.

Elizabeth turned. "I'll be right there," she said. She was at the front of the room with Lila, Ellen, Eva, and Jessica. They were talking about the contest.

"I did all my homework," Lila was saying. "I just have to remember not to whisper during class today."

"Maybe you'll even keep it up after the zookeeper's visit on Monday," Eva said, giggling.

"Fat chance," Ellen said. Lila glared at her. "Well, it's true, Lila. You're not as quiet as Eva and Eliza—"

"I bet Lila won't lose a star today," Jessica spoke up.

"Neither will I," Elizabeth said. "I did all my homework too. Spelling was really easy." She pointed to a sheet of paper lying on top of some books on her desk. It was her spelling homework.

"Elizabeth, are you coming?" Amy yelled from the back again. "Thumbelina is playing with the wheel and she looks so cute."

"OK, OK," Elizabeth said. She ran over to Amy.

Jessica watched her sister go. She was still upset that Elizabeth was getting so much attention from everyone. But there wasn't much she could do about it.

"I'm going to sit down," Jessica told her friends.

"So am I," Lila said. She went to her seat, walking by Elizabeth's desk on the way. That's when Jessica saw Lila pick up a sheet of paper from Elizabeth's desk, rip it up, and throw away the pieces. Lila didn't notice that Jessica was watching her. But Jessica just shrugged and ignored what Lila was doing. She didn't feel like sticking up for Elizabeth right then.

Elizabeth and Amy had finished feeding the hamsters and were coming to sit down too.

"My spelling homework is gone," Elizabeth said, staring at the books on her desk. "It was right on top before. Is it on the floor, Amy?"

"No," Amy answered. "I don't see it. Caroline, have you seen Elizabeth's homework?"

Caroline was standing nearby, talking to

Julie Porter. "Sure," Caroline said. "I saw Lila take it off Elizabeth's desk."

Elizabeth turned to face Lila. "Have you seen my spelling?" Elizabeth asked her.

Lila turned up her nose. "Of course not. Caroline's lying. She probably took it herself."

Caroline put her hands on her hips. "I didn't take it. And I'm not lying, either," she said angrily. "It was Lila. I saw her do it."

"I didn't take Elizabeth's homework," Lila whispered as Mrs. Otis walked into the room. "And you can't prove I did."

Jessica bit her lip. She had seen Lila take it with her own eyes. And she had seen Lila rip up the paper and throw it in the wastebasket. But Jessica still didn't say anything.

"Forget it," Elizabeth told Eva and Amy. "It doesn't matter."

"OK," Eva said slowly. "Lila will probably lose a star whispering anyway."

But Jessica couldn't forget it. Lila had taken

Elizabeth's homework and that wasn't playing fair. Jessica couldn't decide whether to tell on Lila or not. She didn't like seeing her twin get in trouble for something that wasn't her fault, but secretly Jessica was glad Elizabeth was going to lose another star. Jessica didn't want her sister to win the contest.

When it was time for spelling, Mrs. Otis asked each person in the class for his or her homework.

"Lila?"

"Here it is," Lila said, waving her spelling.

"Elizabeth?"

"I–I— don't have mine," Elizabeth said. She didn't mention that her homework had disappeared from her desk.

Mrs. Otis looked surprised. Everyone knew Elizabeth always did her homework. But the teacher walked over to the board and erased one of Elizabeth's stars so that only eight were left.

Lila grinned. She still had nine stars.

Jessica couldn't help smiling a little. Elizabeth was already the center of attention. There was no reason she should get to be assistant zookeeper too.

CHAPTER 8

The Zoo Question

That afternoon Ellen slipped a piece of paper onto Lila's desk. It was a drawing of a tall, very skinny boy. His ears were twice as big as his head. At the bottom of the paper, it said, "The skinniest boy in the world."

Lila giggled. "It's Winston," she whispered.

Mrs. Otis raised her head. She was grading papers at her desk and had not seen that Lila and Ellen had been passing notes for at least five minutes. Then the teacher looked down again.

Ellen passed Lila another note. It said,

"Maybe Winston has big ears because he was an elephant in another life."

Lila burst into laughter. She didn't realize Mrs. Otis was watching her.

"Lila, Ellen," Mrs. Otis said. "That's enough now. Nobody is going to be able to finish their math if you keep disturbing them. Girls, you each just lost a star."

Mrs. Otis went to the board and erased one of Lila's and one of Ellen's stars.

Elizabeth grinned. Now she and Lila each had eight stars.

"It looks as if the contest isn't over yet," Mrs. Otis said.

For the rest of the afternoon, Elizabeth and Lila were as quiet as mice. Time ticked by slowly. But finally, there were only a few minutes before the end of class.

"I think we'd better pick our assistant zookeeper now," Mrs. Otis announced.

"Elizabeth and Lila are still tied for first place."

Lila and Elizabeth sat up straighter in their seats.

"I'm going to ask each of you a question about zoos," Mrs. Otis said. "Whoever gives the best answer wins the contest."

Elizabeth took a deep breath. Her heart was beating fast.

"OK, I'll ask you the first question, Lila," Mrs. Otis said. "What is a nocturnal animal?"

Jessica watched Lila anxiously. That was a hard question—Jessica didn't know the answer herself. She hoped Lila did.

Lila's mouth fell open. "Umm . . ." she said. Then she paused for a long time. "Is it an animal like a woodpecker?" she finally said. "One that knocks on things?"

Elizabeth smiled. She knew the answer

from her library book *Animals in the Zoo*. Lila had guessed wrong.

Mrs. Otis shook her head. "Sorry, Lila. Elizabeth, do you know what a nocturnal animal is?"

"It's an animal that sleeps during the day," Elizabeth answered. "And stays awake all night."

"Exactly right," Mrs. Otis said with a smile. "Very good, Elizabeth. Congratulations. You'll be our assistant zookeeper on Monday."

"Mrs. Otis, that wasn't fair," Jessica called out. "That question was too hard. Lila didn't have a chance."

Mrs. Otis winked at Jessica. "It must not have been *too* hard. Your sister got it right."

Elizabeth had felt happy when she got the answer right. But now she felt sad and angry. She didn't understand why Jessica was being so mean. Elizabeth could tell that Jessica had wanted Lila to win the contest, even though she knew how much Elizabeth wanted to win. *Why is Jessica mad at me?* Elizabeth wondered.

CHAPTER 9

Making Up

When the final bell rang, everyone lined up to go home. "Have a nice weekend, class," Mrs. Otis said.

"I'll try," Elizabeth muttered.

Jessica didn't say anything.

"I can't wait to see the animals on Monday," Ellen told the teacher.

"I can hardly wait either," Mrs. Otis said with a smile.

Elizabeth gathered her books and headed for the bus. Jessica waited until her sister was already down the hall before she started walking. Then on the bus, Jessica sat down next to Caroline.

Elizabeth glanced over at her sister a few times during the ride home, but Jessica pretended not to notice. When the bus arrived at their stop, Jessica was the first one out. She walked quickly to the house and pulled open the door. Elizabeth closed it with a loud bang.

Mrs. Wakefield was sitting in the living room, reading the mail. "Hi, you two."

"Hi," Elizabeth said with a frown.

"Hi," Jessica said, looking down at her feet.

"How was school today?" Mrs. Wakefield asked.

Elizabeth and Jessica shrugged.

Mrs. Wakefield laughed. "A pair of twin thunderclouds have gotten into my house, and their names are Jessica and Elizabeth."

The twins didn't laugh.

"Well, maybe a snack will put you both in a better mood," Mrs. Wakefield said. "Come to the kitchen." While Mrs. Wakefield took out a plate of homemade oatmeal-and-cinnamon cookies, Jessica thought about Elizabeth's cast, and the candy, balloons, cards, and flowers her sister had received. Now she was going to be assistant zookeeper. It just wasn't fair. Jessica bit into a cookie, but she was too angry to enjoy it.

Elizabeth put down her glass of milk. A little spilled over the side.

"Watch it," Jessica yelled.

"How come you're so mad at me?" Elizabeth demanded. "I haven't done anything to you."

"Because!" Jessica exploded.

"Because why?" Elizabeth asked.

"Because . . . you—you—broke your arm!" Jessica said.

One side of Elizabeth's mouth turned up. Then she started to giggle.

For a moment, Jessica looked furious. Then she started to giggle too.

"I'm sorry," Elizabeth managed to say. "I'll try not to do it again."

"Good," Jessica said. "Next time, it's my turn."

"It's a deal," Elizabeth said. "But I don't get it. How come you want to break your arm?"

"It looks like fun," Jessica said. "You got lots of great presents. And everyone at school thought you were a hero."

"I'm not a hero," Elizabeth said. "I'm just clumsy. Hey, do you want some of the candy I got from Grandma and Grandpa now? I saved some for you."

"Definitely," Jessica said.

Mrs. Wakefield smiled. "I knew the cookies would work wonders," she joked. "Now run along. And try not to spoil your appetite completely."

Jessica and Elizabeth ran upstairs to their room. Elizabeth took her box of chocolates out of a drawer and handed it to Jessica.

"Having a broken arm really isn't much fun," Elizabeth said as Jessica popped a chocolate-covered almond into her mouth. "It hurts. And I can't scratch when it itches."

Jessica looked sympathetic. "That must be awful. I'm sorry I was mean to you."

"OK," Elizabeth said. "Friends again?"

"Best friends," Jessica said. "And I'm happy you get to be assistant zookeeper. Lila doesn't know anything about animals."

"She'd probably hold them upside down," Elizabeth said.

"And wonder why they weren't banging their heads against anything," Jessica added, giggling.

"Come on, Jess," Elizabeth said. "Everyone knows only nocturnal animals do that."

They fell onto Elizabeth's bed in a fit of laughter.

CHAPTER 10

Amazing Animals

"Good morning, Ms. Costello," Mrs. Otis said. "We're all very excited to see you. I've had all the desks moved to the sides so that we have plenty of room."

The zookeeper smiled at the teacher and at all of the kids sitting in a circle on the floor. "Please call me Alice, everyone." She set three cages down in the middle of the circle. "Who's going to be my assistant today?"

"Elizabeth is," Jessica called out.

Elizabeth stood up and walked over to Alice. Alice reached down and shook her hand.

"Hello, Elizabeth. Thanks for helping me out. Your job is to keep an eagle eye on the animals while I talk to the class." Alice winked at Elizabeth. "Let me know if anybody tries to escape."

Elizabeth giggled. She knew Alice was just joking.

Alice uncovered the medium-sized cage and carefully lifted out the boa constrictor.

"Wow," Charlie said. "He's huge!"

"This is Captain Crunch," Alice told the class. "He's huge *and* heavy. Elizabeth, would you like to help me hold him?"

Elizabeth held up her cast. "I can only use one hand."

"Hmm," Alice said. "That is a problem. Maybe you can pick someone to help you."

"I pick Jessica," Elizabeth said.

Jessica shook her head. "I don't like snakes."

Elizabeth laughed. "OK. Amy, then."

Amy jumped up. Alice wrapped Captain Crunch around Elizabeth's and Amy's shoulders. The snake's skin was cool and smooth.

"Boas live in tropical climates," Alice said. "They only need about one big meal a month to survive and grow."

"Don't they strangle other animals?" Andy asked.

"Oooh, you better watch out," Todd called out to Elizabeth and Amy. "Maybe Captain Crunch is hungry. He may eat one of you."

Elizabeth looked at Alice. "Is that true?"

The zookeeper shook her head. "Don't be afraid. Boas do strangle their victims, but Captain Crunch isn't hungry right now. He won't hurt you. Actually, many people have boas as pets."

After Alice put Captain Crunch in his cage, she took out the tarantula spider. Elizabeth held the spider in her good hand while her classmates touched it if they wanted to. The tarantula was almost as big as Elizabeth's hand, and it was covered with fur.

"I'm glad I didn't get to be assistant zookeeper," Lila whispered loudly to Jessica. "Tarantulas are the ickiest things ever."

"Now, now, Lila," Mrs. Otis said. "I'll bet Alice doesn't think tarantulas are icky."

Alice laughed. "Not anymore. Tarantulas have a bad reputation as poisonous spiders. But while their bite is painful, it's not dangerous. And they don't bite at all unless they are very, very frightened. There are other spiders that are much more poisonous."

"Well, it's not scared now. It's tickling me," Elizabeth said, as the spider crawled up her arm.

"I hope none of you will be afraid of the last animal I brought," the zookeeper said after she had put the spider back in its cage. She uncovered the biggest of the three cages she had brought. Inside was a baby leopard. Alice

led it out on a leash. The leopard had beautiful blue eyes and big paws.

"Her name is Abby," Alice said. "Her big paws show that she'll be very large when she grows up."

"She's so pretty," Lila said, leaning forward to pet Abby.

Alice let everyone pet the leopard gently.

Winston grinned. "She looks like my cat."

"Do leopards purr?" Todd asked Alice.

"That's a good question," Alice said. "But in fact, most big cats can't purr. And leopards don't roar like lions, either. But they can make a sort of high-pitched yowl when they're frightened or angry."

Alice let everyone look and touch all the animals some more. Then it was time for her to leave. Everyone was sad to see her go, but they had had lots of fun—especially Elizabeth and Jessica. It was great to be best friends again.

                    *   *   *

The next day, Elizabeth, Jessica, Amy, Ellen, Eva, and Lila all ate lunch together. Jessica winked at her sister as Lila opened her
lunch box. Elizabeth winked back and tried
not to laugh.

"What did you bring to eat today?" Jessica
asked Lila.

Lila peeked into her lunch box. "A sandwich, corn chips, and—UGH!" Lila screamed
and threw her lunch box across the cafeteria.

"What's wrong, Lila?" Ellen asked.

Lila's eyes were wide with fear. "There's a
huge spider in my lunch box!"

Elizabeth and Jessica started to laugh.
"Don't worry, Lila. It isn't real," Elizabeth
said.

Lila frowned at Elizabeth for a long moment. Then she got up and stomped over to
where her lunch box had landed. "Very funny,"
Lila muttered to herself.

Ellen looked puzzled. "What just happened?"

"Jessica and I thought Lila needed to learn not to steal other people's homework," Elizabeth explained.

"We decided a visit from an extra-hairy tarantula would teach her," Jessica said.

"Even if it was just a plastic one," Elizabeth added. "There's a note taped on it that says, 'Tarantulas don't like it when you steal.'"

Eva laughed. "Where did you get it?"

"We bought it yesterday at the toy store at the mall," Jessica said. "Elizabeth has some money saved up from Christmas."

Lila came and sat back down. She started eating her sandwich without a word.

"I'm going to buy something else with the rest of my Christmas money," Elizabeth told her friends. "I want to get that new video game called Goin' Wild."

"Isn't that the game Andy's always playing?" Amy asked.

"Yeah," Elizabeth said. "It's really fun."

Jessica made a face. "I think it's boring."

"Just wait until I get one," Elizabeth told her sister. "You'll like it."

Jessica crossed her arms in front of her chest. "I doubt it."

Will a video game come between Jessica and Elizabeth? Find out in Sweet Valley Kids #36, ELIZABETH'S VIDEO FEVER.

SWEET VALLEY KIDS

Jessica and Elizabeth have had lots of adventures in *Sweet Valley High* and *Sweet Valley Twins*...now read about the twins at age seven! You'll love all the fun that comes with being seven—birthday parties, playing dress-up, class projects, putting on puppet shows and plays, losing a tooth, setting up lemonade stands, caring for animals and much more! It's all part of SWEET VALLEY KIDS. Read them all!

- [ ] **BEST FRIENDS #1** .... 15655-1/$3.25
- [ ] **TEACHER'S PET #2** .... 15656-X/$2.99
- [ ] **THE HAUNTED HOUSE #3** .... 15657-8/$2.99
- [ ] **CHOOSING SIDES #4** .... 15658-6/$2.99
- [ ] **SNEAKING OUT #5** .... 15659-4/$3.25
- [ ] **THE NEW GIRL #6** .... 15660-8/$3.25
- [ ] **THREE'S A CROWD #7** .... 15661-6/$3.25
- [ ] **FIRST PLACE #8** .... 15662-4/$3.25
- [ ] **AGAINST THE RULES #9** .... 15676-4/$3.25
- [ ] **ONE OF THE GANG #10** .... 15677-2/$2.99
- [ ] **BURIED TREASURE #11** .... 15692-6/$3.25
- [ ] **KEEPING SECRETS #12** .... 15702-7/$3.25
- [ ] **STRETCHING THE TRUTH #13** .... 15654-3/$3.25
- [ ] **TUG OF WAR #14** .... 15663-2/$3.25
- [ ] **THE OLDER BOY #15** .... 15664-0/$3.25
- [ ] **SECOND BEST #16** .... 15665-9/$2.75
- [ ] **BOYS AGAINST GIRLS #17** .... 15666-7/$3.25
- [ ] **CENTER OF ATTENTION #18** .... 15668-3/$2.75
- [ ] **THE BULLY #19** .... 15667-5/$2.99
- [ ] **PLAYING HOOKY #20** .... 15606-3/$3.25
- [ ] **LEFT BEHIND #21** .... 15609-8/$2.99
- [ ] **OUT OF PLACE #22** .... 15628-4/$3.25
- [ ] **CLAIM TO FAME #23** .... 15624-1/$2.75
- [ ] **JUMPING TO CONCLUSIONS #24** .... 15635-7/$2.75
- [ ] **STANDING OUT #25** .... 15653-5/$2.75
- [ ] **TAKING CHARGE #26** .... 15669-1/$2.75

Buy them at your local bookstore or use this handy page for ordering:

Bantam Books, Dept. SVT3, 2451 S. Wolf Road, Des Plaines, IL 60018

Please send me the items I have checked above. I am enclosing $_____
(please add $2.50 to cover postage and handling). Send check or money
order, no cash or C.O.D.s please.

Mr/Ms _____

Address _____

City/State _____ Zip _____

SVT3-12/92

Please allow four to six weeks for delivery.
Prices and availability subject to change without notice.